© 2016 by Deep Rivers and King Judah . All rights reserved.
Published by Vantage Point Publishing
Indianapolis, IN 46205

ISBN 978-1-943159-06-2

The publisher would appreciate notification where errors occur so that they may be corrected in subsequent printing and/or editions. Please send comments to the publisher by emailing to deeprivers67@yahoo.com

Printed in the United States of America

Shattered but Not Broken

by

King Judah & Deep Rivers

SHATTERED BUT NOT BROKEN :
WOUNDED

KING

The twisted sea of love
has brought me to this conclusion
that before I can hold your hand
I must get out of this illusion

I am broken by the stranglehold of love
it has me in fear that I will never meet the
right one
the anger, the misconceptions, the lack of
attention
the fights, the arguments have left me with
resentment

I am WOUNDED
fractured by a woman's lies to my heart
that I barricade my feelings behind this pain
blocking my love for ever getting hurt again

Failed relationship after another
thinking that one loves me but only with a
fork tongue

to there is no equivalent to this barrier so
wrong
that is why I do not know if I ever will fall
in love

I want you to know that I am Wounded
a man that looks at you and says she is
perfect
but afraid you will consider my confession
to be passive
yet, to me it is a part of my life's lesson

Can you really love a WOUNDED man?
and put the right effort to really truly
understand
it is not my will to be like this in no way
but this is who I am. WOUNDED
I am SHATTERED but not BROKEN
but yet I needed to tell you
where I am at in this hour - in this moment

DEEP RIVERS

The rivers that I have drowned in all my life..
Contained my memories of pain and strife...
The reality that eludes most...but fills my lungs
with
ash of frustration...
As I constantly suffer at the hands of humiliation
and condemnation

Love the one catalyst that covers my eyes
A heart that loves deep and responsible for my
demise...

To love again...a question that I know not the
answer
and run from the thought of....
Wounded, struck like lightning...tossed across
the rivers

That I continue to drown in.....all my life

For each moment that I live....I slowly die
From broken bones to blackened eyes

Giving love from the depths of ones soul only to
have
reality snatch it back and toss it once again

and again...and again....and again

Do I continue to look for love or allow love to

find me
Or should I hide and live in my own fantasy of
what ifs
Moments of colored glass seconds that only
when you remove them the same story remains

Shackled by the truth that I want
to...love....need to be loved and then once
again....nothing

How could one soul be so wrong...battered and
bruised by lies and confusion...the heart that
cries but stuck in an illusion of no one loves a
WOUNDED soul....broken beyond repair...so I
hide...

The wounds that constantly burn as the reality
is...
My broken life....an everlasting reality....of a love
gone wrong

And I keep wanting.....

SHATTERED BUT NOT BROKEN (Can it be repaired)
Chapter 2

DEEP RIVERS

My soul is stuck on repeat
lost in the battle of why me
and yes over and over again
damn...the same song
different man
hurt
belittled and humiliation
has became my friend
and I forgive
to take the next step
never holding his mess against the next
love is real and I feel it deep
to be caressed...kissed...and held
through the winds of the storm
can this ever happen for me

I stare in the mirror
at the scars that whisper
I do not deserve
and I scream back...why...
but I already know the answer
it must be me...not the beauty I see
the warmth that I possess
the knowledge I give
the love that makes you scream my name
because you screamed...someone name that

wasn't mine

The ugly that resides in my heart
must be what everyone sees..
a smile that lights the sky..
with tears that stream from my reality
a wounded soul..
shattered not broken...
can it be repaired
the cycles of abuse
not new to me..
but now time to leave me
or am I just broken?

KING

The deepness of my soul
Is bruised beyond recognition
It's misplaced
Out of position
Been a sucker for love
Now my walls are up
Inside I hide me in a prison
Afraid to make a love connection

This hurt has become my cancer
Spreading throughout my spirit like wildfire
And now I'm at a place where I want to be free
Can you be that balm for me?
My shattered pieces are a fraction of my reality
I've
 been used like meat just for money
Thought this woman loved me
But killed me totally inwardly

My dream became nightmares
I sat in the darkness in my tears
Battered as a wounded man
Dead of feelings for any woman
LOOK AT ME IF YOU DARE!!!
My smile won't tell you how I been played
So now to others it looks like I'm playing games
But, CAN they understand my story my way?
Look at me... if...you can
Scared

Shattered

SHATTERED BUT NOT BROKEN
Chapter 3

DEEP RIVERS

I have been physically, mentally, verbally abused
and such.....
molested, raped and no longer trust.....
the scars that whisper....
loudly but never heard.....
the vanishing colors of the bruises....
seen but never spoken.....
as the remnants of my trust....
blows in the wind....
of yesterday's storm....
how, why and when.....
at the turn of the clock....
my existence my sin....
and I still rise...
with the power of desire....
hope and determination....
no longer room for hesitation....
as the once wounded child....
grasp hold....to trust the heart.....
with the words that flow from the depth of pain....
My Power is mine all over again.....
the battle to win and never give up....
my battle of life....

KING

I stand at the road where you had departed
to help repair the things that we have broken
the colors that are on your skin
comes from the bruises deep within
My stubbornness caused us to drift apart
yes, I did not want to understand your heart
a man stuck deep in his own quicksand
becoming cold and disrespectful because of my
pain

You molested my mind to make me believe
that you raping my heart was nothing but reality
you did it so well and very naturally
you became my vicious nightmare instead of my
dream
My wounds are longer than Nile River
the vapor of you still moisten my lips
I cringe inside is how you used me to no end
and you did it unmercifully time and time again

Where there is an action there is a reaction
and there is no way I can play the innocent
I caused a lot of storms because I did not know
who I was
my mind shut down way before my heart
Shattered in many tiny pieces
splattered like a rose trampled on the ground
you accused me and I accused you
we blame each other and we forget about the
truth

I'm...
splashed oil
mixed with water
I am a ink blot
specks
spluttered
whoosh
a rushing sound
shattered
but not Broken

SHATTERED NOT BROKEN

Chapter 4

DEEP RIVERS

Education....
manipulation.....
with constant stipulations....
bring about revelations.....
that may come....
illusion...
delusion...
confusion....
that cause so many intrusions.....
and then silence....
words that are spoken......
promises that are broken.....
am I just a token......
or that of value or worth.....
stepped on like the dirt....
forgotten like an unfinished meal.....
or pieces of my heart to steal......
the continuous battle in my mind....
peace to find.....
retreating to the grind....
of a mission to see.......
the lines written but still not complete......
the words are racing.....
constantly pacing.....
through the walls of my soul......
to capture happiness...
my true goal.....

the power to hear my cries....
.listen to my words.....
my forbidden sigh....

KING

Misunderstanding
uncaring
no reaction
living in depression
For fear has gripped me
banishing me to my own Island
my own strength screams in silence
my tainted heart all I do is hide it

Confusion
delusions
confrontation with actual facts
a fixed false belief that believes she would come
back
The resistant to reason
a paranoid intrusion
what a misleading opinion
that I believed time and time again

When I finally listened
I heard my own cries
then I finally was able to cry
to peeked at my own pain hidden inside

She controlled me
be it unknowingly to me
maybe I did not want to see
but I purposed my heart to...believe

SHATTERED BUT NOT BROKEN ~ THE PROCESS
Chapter 5

KING

I am a man processing information
recording and making notations on my pain
following up with appropriate action
so I won't live in anymore illusions
My past love still dictates to me
she is haunting my future dreams
I fell in love as the ocean is deep
it left me broken and shattered on my knees

"The caged bird sings
with a fearful trill
of things unknown
but longed for still
and his tune is heard
on the distant hill
for the caged bird
sings of freedom."
-Maya Angelou

Release me
Free me
Stop Whispering
I am not listening
For now I am finding shelter
in a Tower that is Higher then I
even though as a man
I still have to break the silence and cry

My test
my storm
my weakness
I will share with you
Will you
console me
hold me
or chastise me
and then judge me

All I ask is that you open the cage
I'll wear the shame
just discard me from your name
there is a new dawn awaits me
I just fell in love with the wrong person
that is part of the journey
It is all part of the process

DEEP RIVERS

A woman trapped in a little girl's nightmare...
Mind captured in the darkness...
Thoughts trapped in the detriment of what was.....
A foundation never built...
In search of a solution...as the hurt inflicts
delusion....
Overflowing illusion...with continuous pain of a
contusion....
So I drop to my knees....Lord Keep Me close....
Whispers...
Whispers...
Peace be Still...Peace be Still....Peace be Still...
I repeat your words as they rest in my soul....
Tears steam as the pain is plenty...
My screams escape...
Why me Lord....Why me Lord...Why me....
Whispers....
Whispers...
My child....fear not...
I will never leave you nor forsake...I am always by
your side....
I am the light of your salvation....
When all else fails...or walks away...
Trust and know that I am forever here....
My love is everlasting....I am the light that forever
shines...
Lord thank you for keeping me close....

THE CONVERSATION: SHATTERED BUT NOT
BROKEN
Chapter 6

KING

I stand in my darkness

Alone
alone
alone
alone

I look at the mirror
all I can see is me
the face that feels incomplete
the voice can do nothing but scream

I stand in my darkness
afraid of my own tears
me and darkness
I cannot see me
Can you see me?
please tell me
please
for I am sitting her alone
standing in my darkness

Deep Rivers: The eyes that see even in
darkness....the voice that is heard over the
screams...and even in silence....never alone...

King: Did I forgive the worst part of me...is the darkness nothing but a man call me....silence....do you hear my heart strings playing...the song of my pain

Deep Rivers : The pain that only last for as long as we hold on to it.....releasing what was....to seek what is......forgiveness the greatest part.....of loving the eyes that stare back.....replacing the song of pain.....with the sunshine of life......

King Judah :I release into your hand...my soul...as a dove being set free...will you hold...the very sacred blemish of my past....to mend and heal...for I can learn to say the words I love you again

Deep Rivers :To take flight.....mended....made whole....the past is just that....the past....it cannot travel into our future.....as it to has been set free.....and the ink will spill once again......and the will appear......it will read.....I love you.....

King Judah : I fight within...inwardly I am split...where is truth...where is you...who is me?...I wonder...looking

Deep Rivers :The battle continues....not
split...but healing one day at a time.....to
become whole.....the truth lies within....the
strength to win......as the thought to
lose.....would be to give up....and there's so
much to do......we are.....the power...behind our
words.....

King Judah :The way you talk to me is like you
know the deepest of the balm that I need.
you know the inward pain and outward joys
knowing that you understand the mountains and
the valleys
let me know that this conversation has been
worth it all

Deep Rivers :A conversation....words
exchanged.....emotions that walk the same
path....the road of darkness.....into
light....valleys that have endless
depth.....mountains that peak into nowhere.....a
conversation.....as you know....I know.....we
know.....words of silence.....

King Judah :I cannot release the total burden of
my plight on your shoulders
the distance between my pain and me afraid of
being hurt again
is still close to each other for the unwrapping
but it is not the wallpaper that I wear on my

heart anymore
but it is a wound that is still healing and
conforming
I am evolving as a man again
but with the giving of myself to love again
is a story that is still in the making

Deep Rivers :The release has begun...the ink
spilled...I am the ears that see.....the eyes that
hear....what has been spoken.....cried
out.....poured in the rivers of
understanding......we walk....forward.....the
story.....not different......the same.....different
time.....same rhythm....same rhyme......to
eventually feel again....live to love again....and
yes.....to share.......the path of
ink...spilled...designed.....so we shall follow...

King Judah : Never falling apart
Because your heart doesn't
Know you at all
Just let your heart grow wings and fly
No pain in wanting to know
just only pain in never letting it show
Just let it explode
And it will find your soul mate that shows

Deep Rivers :The ink that floats to the
pages.....verses that read the hearts

depth.....and truest emotions.....ink of the hearts......

Chapter 7

KING JUDAH

You called me at the right time I was thinking about you all night and then it Dawned on me I am in love with the thought of starting anew

The shattered pieces had their season now I see the twinkle of hope again with you will you please don't take this as being forward with you my head is never lowered

I fought through the hedges of thorny love being pricked by all types of past pain and stains with others all I could do was pretend but you took my hand and there was no blot of sin

You saw past the wounds and looked at the visible scars the sinking sand of judgment was not an opinion for you knew the struggle because you had your own then you reached in my life and kissed my soul

So, as I gaze in your eyes I must declare that I love you more in each passing day and I crown you the royal desire of my life please take me slow as nothing I will hide

You hold the moments of my future so clear as I stand here naked with no shame anymore I have exposed to you my deepest inner chamber let me resolve that on this day my love for you no longer is shattered

Logic has build a home for my mind to settle that my brokenness is nothing short but experience so

as you teach ~ I learn and I bow to the knowledge
of you that really does burn

DEEP RIVERS

The Dawn rises each and every day...

Bringing new dreams new hope....the start of anew

The shattered pieces that fall across the rivers of
deep waters

With a chance of rain and the ability to restore
what was and what can be

The light that shines at the end of the tunnel

A kiss that allows fireworks to burn

You made me learn

My worth more precious than gold

Giving more than a whisper but the opportunity to
move into something new

That which holds the heart...breath of new life

Lessons learned that give decisions on what path
to take

The life that was is now beckoning to start and
fulfill all that we make

To walk forward and never look backwards as life
has given me a fresh new storm

To ride the wave of ecstasy

Allowing the twinkle in your eye to glisten

Brighter than the past and the sun that shines
upon us

A smile that lights the room with the smoothness
of silk

Yes I have walked the path of shattered and
broken

But I am not the common token

I am priceless

And those that gaze into my eyes see the light

Those that read my words

Read the power that they possess

And those that need the healing

Seek to find...and find what heals the soul

Giving hope to the spirit of moving forward

A love that returns with the motive of being free

And showering you with all that your heart desires

Yes I was once broken and then you gave me hope

Showed me the possibilities

Enforced my value and worth

You made my emotions move heaven and earth

As you showed more than appreciation

That started from birth

You gave me hope to once again

Fly free and value me....

SHATTERED NOT BROKEN
Chapter 8

KING JUDAH

Will you hold me in my disappointments?
for that is when you become my friend
and not solely my sexually lover
but one that will go to no end
For as I mend in the fragile fragments
I want to look in your eyes and kiss my tomorrow
I want to be able to be sensitive without regret
giving you my vulnerable side even in my lack
The nectar of your heart is my sweetest juice
for I peel your thoughts to kiss the center
for your greatest greatness is stimulating
and very profound and rewarding
I need you to connect with me emotionally
to understand the mountains that I have climbed
the deep rivers that almost drown me
and the lowness of all my valleys
The dew of your mist is so refreshing
for you have a calmness about you that is effective
your confidence is never low outwardly
but even in your low moments I adore you
I give you my soft spots
torn, broken, shattered and frizzle
you never try to give me a muzzle
could you be that piece missing in my puzzle?

DEEP RIVERS

To hold and never let go...
through trials and tribulations...
across the sea of revelation...a true friend is
always there...
more than a lover....a spirit that will stand in the
rain
as we both gain
the understanding of disappointments that are
lessons of pain
ability to mend so much more than fragments of
yesterday
Today is tomorrows foundation
steadily building what can be
lips that carry the sweetest nectar
as words escape the nectar spills into the
atmosphere
of the valleys that hold desire
splashed across the rivers needing
more than a moment less than a second
the love that continues to build...one brick at a
time
broken yes...shattered....many times
put back together to soar once again
as the sun rises my eyes hear
and my ears see
my true reality....
yes the friendship that travels through a broken
that holds the pieces together to be
given a new meaning...

pieces of the puzzle that allow the calm
to appear once again...

SHATTERED BUT NOT BROKEN~The Love Storm
Chapter 9

JUDAH

I rolled over to turn the light on the nightstand
as yesterday argument became an instant replay
she called and the memories was displayed on
your face
the confining wall of jealousy engulfed our love
space
I saw it brewing before a word was even spoken
You think I don't feel the hurt that ached your
heart
the pain that you go through with the mental wars
and the emotional roller-Coaster makes it hard
Every person that I have dated is not an enemy to
our love
I cannot stand in these unexplored waters moving
towards a storm
insecurities has never been the right prescription
for us
for we gathered twigs and branches to build up our
trust
Our tress of faith is swaying from the gust of
unsure persuasion
yet I am standing firm as I lay here in bed that our
love is true
worthy of confidence is my mindset about this
dubious faltering
when the phone rang I didn't have any guilt
because I love who I am with

The Love Storm
the angry sea of unconvincing doubt of what could
be
we either ride this wave together or part as friends
I am not sure where this storm will lead or will it
ever end
I did not once asked you to tell Dajuan not to call
you
for I know when I would wake it was me beside
you
Keshawn, Daniel, even Manny your kid's father
I treated them with manhood when their
childishness was cruel
I welcome your children to the world of love and
warmth
now you are making me face a hell of a storm
check yourself...I never cause you to disbelieve
I am going back to bed and just act like this is a
damn dream

DEEP RIVERS

As the pillows are tossed around....and the sleep
seems to invade me....a hour here a hour
there...and the thoughts just continue to race
through my mind
I keep asking and pleading with myself...and the
answers just don't
come...compromising...calculating what went
wrong...what wasn't right
and the constant visual continues to play....how
can this continue to happen to me...the lies
told...the kisses so bold...that drew me all the way
back in
My senses never are wrong...even when I don't
listen to them....follow my so called woman's
intuition....but your kiss drew me back in
You try to convince once again that I am the one
you love....and the past is just that the past...you
say I come first but how...is that...
You called me her name...you were seen having
lunch once again...and it was not me or your
mother....and my vision is not deceiving me...the
one being deceived is you...
See the reality of the situation is that no
matter...the lies...you tell...the flowers...you
bring...the loving that you think...will make me
forget...once again....
You missed the words that slipped from my
lips....yes I toss and turn...and sleep only for a
short while...but at this moment...you are not
sleeping at all....

I suddenly wake and realize...that I have had the
nightmare....that will soon become yours....as I
push replay....as soon as the sun comes up....
But for now...I will grab my pillows...and see if I
can't see....how this nightmare ends....

SHATTERED NOT BROKEN
Chapter 10

KING JUDAH

In the shadow of the morning is your face

lovely, existing and so radiant

I am here to tell you that my day has just began

with thoughts of your love surrounding me

I know my broken pieces maybe tiny slithers

but in you there is a peace that gives me wisdom

that teaches me to mend with prayer and
thanksgiving

for in the presence of you is the greatest fulfillment

You took my fragments and examined them with
love

broken, torn, weary, heart bleeding and minced

but with a calming spirit and a smooth hand

you wash my dirty past and claim me as your only
man

I have to remind myself why you love me

broken relationship after another

comparing you to the next woman

yet you stood with a precious heart of gold

I am awe of you and I cannot say how much you
have

refreshed me

I know that I am in love with you like a love feast

for you are my favorite recipe and everything that I will

ever need

I bow to you in the presence of angels as you take my

hand

I am better

even in the state of mending

I am in love

for your hands are receiving

Your kiss

your touch

your life

is the true meaning of our healing

DEEP RIVERS

In the shadows of what was has now become the present

The broken pieces slowly are becoming relevant in the place

Of wholeness...completion...to start over again

Not in the same place but a new foundation

That no longer holds humiliation

Of a constant fall down and get up and fall down and get up

The realization that each piece...

Had to be examined...evaluated ....and then silence

To be evaluated again....the purpose to learn a lesson

Sometimes many lessons needed to go forward

The past is just that...the dirty lens

Cleansed to shine...

Love shared that is the whisper in the night

When the tears fall with no eyes around to see

This is my reality...

As I drop to my knees

Head held high....

I scream...and ....scream...and scream

With a flow of tears

That are for you...to pray and pray

Lord ! hear me as I come to you and ask for your ear

Once again

I plead my case for the broken but not shattered

Torn but able to be mended

To heal a cold heart with your warmth as you have mine

Many Many times...

Hear what he cannot see...and see what he cannot hear

And wrap him in your loving arms...to know

That yes it was broken...but not shattered as the pieces learned

Their rightful place again....

Better than before...

That is love....

SHATTERED BUT NOT BROKEN ~ UNDERCOVER
LOVER
Chapter 11

KING

How dare you tell me you love me
then when I come over by surprise
you are cuddling with Jodi
is this a nightmare or a dream

After all the stress I shared with you
after you saying you love me and know me
then I get the eye opener of horror
that you really had an Undercover Lover

I am strong but you hit my sensitivity
breaking the mended pieces to mini fragments
I thought you really loved this brother
but yet you pushed our love away for this
Undercover Lover

I am not bitter at the treatment that I did not
deserve
I am just confused at this matter that came my
way
my heart hurts and my mind is sunken in despair
all I was doing is building love for our atmosphere

In the sea of this abyss I fall and don't know if I
will survive
I lost another piece of me that I thought was fixed

but I once again learn a lesson that is not call love
this time I can admit that I really had enough

But before I go I want to let you know one thing
my power is sapped and life is dwindled
but I will not feel guilty or even suffer
you go ahead and enjoy your Undercover Lover

DEEP RIVERS

I listen....and listen
I want to scream as this is not what I am supposed
to be hearing
but I am....

Hell I want to scream to the rooftop
I want to be silent and let it hurt
and then I just want to simply walk away

We really are not at this place...are you serious
all the late night calls
all the long walks and talks in the park
and I ask myself are we really back here

Did you take me to a place of hurt yet once again
I ask because...not only does it open your wounds
but your wounds are not alone...
the spill that fell from the mountain top
when you fell you took me with you...

And now I am the cushion to break the fall

I answered your questions night after night....and
you know
Love don't love nobody when you don't love you...

Damn the words....the actions splattered in red
allover
Or are you all of a sudden colorblind?

step by step we were walking to the path of
restoration
healing the hurt
lowering the volume on the scream to a whisper
and you moved too fast

you looked in the mirror of fantasy and did not see
death that stared back at you
she took you all the way back...she wants you him
and whoever else she can have...or will you listen
to her lies

And you fell for the lines for the last damn time
I will not stand by and watch you fall again.....
this is the last time
My dearest friend

I drop to my knees yet again
I scream to the mountain top....not just for you but
for all those
that can't see the forest for the trees

you are so much more than the surface
the value goes deep and the worth priceless
but before you will ever know you have to see you
for you
love who you are not for what was

Nothing stays undercover for long
as the sun is surely to rise
her ass surely got set....

And you blame me for what I did......

you walked away first, never to walk that way
again.....

my favorite game.....checkmate...

SHATTERED BUT NOT BROKEN: I FELT THE WIND
Chapter 12

KING JUDAH

I felt the wind that moved the trees
the breeze came in the presence of you
love became a instinct reality again
at the point where I felt hopeless to no end

I saw your eyes gazing at the soul of my life
you saw the pain and the marking of my scars
you reached out in the the storm of my weakness
to try to grab my hand and build my trust again

I tried to push pass the brink of my
discouragement
and focus on the meaning of the your eyes
for I wanted to see what you saw in me
pass fossil rock mentality and disguise

Do you see the history of my hurt?
look closely at the dents of my open wounds
for I cannot even cover them with a bandage
I just function and try so hard to manage

Still waters pass at my feet like quiet sheep
I see the forest green trees compass about me
struggling to deal with the demise of yesterday
healing
to deal with today's reality of being numbed

The slight touch of you gives me goose bumps

for even though I don't see you I feel you
mentally I am drained trying to harvest a new crop
of love
I cannot tell the wheat from the tares in the field
of obstacles

Your eyes meets me in the shadow of my morning
developing the sunset of a beautiful aftermath of
faith
I take in the picture of the romantic view of you
you kissed me in the midst of this dubious dew

Quietly I fashion myself to release the brokenness
to reveal the shatter pieces of my spoils
for I know in me there is a tissue and issues that
need repair
It is in this wind you understand this constant fear

DEEP RIVERS

The history of your hurt worn in your eyes
A smile that is upright but does not disguise the
lies
of loneliness and heartache
You fool me but never the eyes the stare pass into
your soul
I constantly see what has been done
Damage that most think is beyond repair
But never an issue for love to love again
Forgiveness at the brink of what almost was
See I am so much more than what you bargained
for
The silent friend that listens more than you say
The warmth, when your soul has been treated so
cold
I am more than a blanket on a cold night
Or fresh lemonade caught in a summer breeze
See, so many forsake the one that stands in the
shadows
Tears fall and no one sees
Even when the tears are for you and not me
The bond that is never broken
and friendship more than any common token
The fashion that never goes out of style
the tears that cleanse the soul
the hope that all can be repaired, restored and
renewed
casting all fear into deep waters....

SHATTERED NOT BROKEN ~ We Will Make It
Work
Chapter 13

KING

Shatter splinters of feelings jostled
ripped into shreds and right off the cuff
minutes pass into sand of an hour glass
holding time with our hearts in tender hands

Through all the rain that has beat upon our
soul
midnight became a friend without the angelic
chorus
I craved you in the presence of my abyss
down spiral
yet you held me close and your love followed

Broken solitude of a serene goddess
like the battered ship on a raging sea ranting
I hear your voice so clear and I am drawn to
your space
I reach out to cup your cheeks and behold
your face

Take me to the magical strength that you
process
mold me into a carved statue that awaits your
arrival
for in the midst of your queenly nature, I see

your tears
like of can of peaches you are the syrup that I
need

Now I invite you to lay with me on white sand
We Made It Work so celebrate with your King
for I am honor to throw my crown at your feet
and dance to your halo forever because you
are my dream

We Made It Work
with power and understanding
We Made It Work
with hope for tomorrow and with a special
loving

DEEP RIVERS

I have never given up…
But I will walk away…never to return…
The battle that was, I have my lessons
learned…
the lines that almost catapulted what we had into
grains of sand
Shattered glass that was the sidewalk beneath
me
Feel what I feel…
Not possible if all you see is you…only things
felt is yours…
Leave you if only for a moment, and walk with
me….
See my forest for the trees…
As the moments continue to flow by as you now
see more than the single blossom upon the hill
You gaze into bushels of blossoming orchids
that breathe life
The sun that is shining ever so bright
the waterfall that cascades below….flowing like
the tears that once was
Not a moment to spare for what stands before
you….
And I breathe…
Deep and slow…
And you fall in sync…..
The sweet sounds of chirping birds with the
whistling of a single humming bird in the
background
Yes the sound of a new day a beginning of what

we made work
What we never gave up on
The melodic whispers of my heart
All the steps driven as the pain forgiven
To know that what is for me will always be...
Regardless of what others may say.....
My unconditional love starts here and now to
stay...
The mystical touch that enthralls our souls
the fire that burns deep in the heart of the
Queen...
The path I live...chiseled out for my craft...
To grow and discern...
Those that are for me and those that never
see....
The lesson to learn as we walk the road to
destiny.....
I am never a dream...
Reality sweeter than honey...with the craving of
nectar....
We made it Work....and the battle won....

DEEP RIVERS

Time has crept on without me once again

Those around me needed and now need no
more

The calculated moves that seem to be
continuous

You walk away as if

I will always sit and wait for the obvious to
be seen

Positivity stuck in the shadows of negativity

And all because I inherited the garage of so
many

Giving them the ability to inhale and exhale

While I drown on a sip of fictitious water
doing what I continue to do

Blaming no one but my self

The heart that takes everyone hurt away

Hidden in my closest so that you can walk
into your greatness

The past is just that for you

The new mountains to climb with the sky as
your limit

And know you have no more negativity

Erased, given to the one that is always there

You purged until the air lifted you into what
is yours, a lighted future

As I took it all so that you could breathe

Not realizing the more I allowed you to
purge the more weighted I became

But isn't that what friends are for

Your hurt was so great that I literally and
physically could feel the same pain

And it was way too great for my friend

So I listen

And listen

And listen

To the moment where the air you breathe is
as sweet as fresh honey

And the smile has returned

You thank me and in seconds ……gone

No need for me

Tossed away like last week's trash

Used up like a whore of the night

No one ever knows

My gift to relieve the pain of others is my
pain in the end…..

KING

Screams, screams,screams the voices you hear
from those who do not care like fallen leaves dying
in the summer heat I walked because there was no
words to speak

The overcast of so much negative rapid utterance
cluttering the filters of my mind that I could not
think a purposeless way to watch the shadows grip
you into fear I wanted to reach my hand out but I
thought you would not care

The blame game of decades of this deplorable
condition are you telling me that you really finally
listened to my silence Broken is the cord that
bounded us together Shattered is the voice of
reason that always matter

Walk in the my valleys and then I will understand
your new mountains you were the new plant that
had been added into my life but the upkeep was
despicable and very wretched how many ways can
I say that I do regret it

I look at everything as the whole movie is being
played how can you say you were used like a
whore in the night have you forgotten from whence
we both came and how much joy and pleasure
were truly gain

Please, don't invite me to no more pity parties for
what you locked in the closet is the heart of you the
reason I fell in love with you from day one come
and walk with me again as a flower under the sun

Others is not your pain for you have become your
pain in the inside toss those feelings back in the
abyss of forgiveness for I know you and your
strength is just a little weaken

SHATTERED NOT BROKEN

Chapter 15

DEEP RIVERS

Broken was your heart

Shattered the belief that love can come again

And the darkness that you chose to walk in
disappeared as quickly as the sun rises

Guaranteed to be

Never stuck in what was but evaluating what
can be

See the ears that listen

Also see that which condones the behaviors
of a broken soul

But never completely beyond a repaired
heart

I held your hand through your darkest days

Felt the beats of your heart when the rhythm
was beyond comprehension

Stuck on repeat at times

And I want to touch it just right to get the beat back on track

I couldn't dance to the melody that was on repeat in my head

And the tighter I held your hand the faster it went

Was it trying to tell me the obvious or was it trying to escape

And at that point my beat was lost

Trying to evaluate the situation that had become a complication

Of me, you or us

Not wanting to fuss

I needed to release, let go of

You took this as a pity party

And once again misunderstood

Misread and almost mislead

But I recuperate and set the record straight

See the vision before you

Listen to the sound of the sultry voice that soothes your soul

The hand that touches you with heat that almost burns

But feels too

Good to let go

I am who I am and yes at time even I need to release

So many weighted with the troubles of the world

My gift to alleviate what pressure I can

To be the listening ear of reason

And yes some do take advantage but that's okay

Always remember each day …..I am just being me

The mystery that really isn't a mystery at all….

KING

I got caught up into my own emotions for I love you
just the way you are but you have been sounding
like a complete stranger and I am trying to be a
rescue ranger

Come inside my life and lets begin where
mysteries has ended for I am examining this from
the seat of your heart I am going to fix us some tea
and we sit in the living room from this point on we
must get this matter unglued

You are not invisible and neither am I invincible
These days, however, the once seemingly eternal
flame and honest aspects of our lives has
architecture our defenses and has caused to
cherished the rubble of our existence

Surely, these statements requires a solution we are
dealing with choices of action that is very difficult
either for an individual or for society at large yet, I
am willing to help make a plan that will not be hard

Right after any tragedy, many people expressed a
defiant resolve to rebuild their lives to be ready for
any lingering trouble we must go back to faith and
truth to guide us it is no secret we are lacking in
the great word call trust

Foundations can be renewed and walls revived I
really care about both of our personal rigid lives but
I am only going to build this house again with you
for it is you that knows how to complete every room

Ears are open my consistent rainbow that never
hides we make each other better and shelter each
other from so many storms I awake to this promise
of grabbing you into the new day of hope for we
must take our vision and use it like it is our only
dope

" love me as if tomorrow will never come

Caressing away the pain of yesterday

Listen to my silence as it tells a story

That searches for the purpose

Of Being

I am

More than the eyes can see

You will know

When you listen"......

           Deep Rivers

SHATTERED NOT BROKEN~ AND....HE THOUGHT~"THE SITUATION"

Chapter 16

KING

A distressing sensation
the emotional suffering
an laborious devotion
in this intoxicated moment

A therapist is far beyond my reach
IF I RELEASE MY THOUGHTS RIGHT
NOW
you will think I lost my mind
lol...I guess I have this time

For you have caused me the worst hurt
broken my heart was the straw in this
world
I seen it with my eye and my ears heard
everything
so no matter what you have to say,
nothing will be the same

You could of told me that our time

passed
I knew something was strange with your
secret plights
private telephone calls during the wee
hours of night
cause I never said anything I guess you
thought everything was alright

I would never thought in a million years
that you would...
well, the signs were there but I ignored
them because I love you
sitting around here playing BooBoo the
fool
for I just couldn't believe this was true

So, I followed you along the Boardwalk
as you sat on the beach and held
another hand
gave away the soft lips that I loved to
kiss
yes that melons lips gloss I could not
resist

I remember how your eyes stared at me
what you could not believe, that it was
me

Just remember that injured feelings
can be much more lastingly hurtful than
physical pain

Then you notice me and it was like I
wasn't there
you lost all your senses without a care
as you gave someone else my world
Just tell me why it had to be another girl

DEEP RIVERS

A situation
That brought complications
from you
none that needed in my view

I sat and pondered
Appropriately reaching for the correct
response
This took time as you had already
condemned me
Thrown away so quickly

I will address each dagger that you
threw
And then I will sit and wait patiently
For the apology that is rightfully do
To me as I did not deserve the shade
you spew

You have the audacity to mention a
therapist
That which I am
And you mock my work
As if you don't give a damn

See your hurt is caused not by me but
the words
That swirl around in your head
Not taking the time needed to simply
just ask
In a matter of seconds you caused all
that we had built to crash

Falling in the sea of no return
As if you were in this all by yourself
Never thinking of anyone else
Just pure selfish

But because of your actions you ask me
why
Did I stare at you the way I did and just
walk on by
Your actions was all that needed to be
said
So I walked head high with a dagger in
my back

See from the moment I met you I said
that we were forever and a day
But you contemplated and manipulated
your thoughts into this
Something that was destined you turned

into a mess
I digress

I said I would address and not get any
more angry than I already am
Damn you
It hurts to think that you think so little of
me
Of us

Or did you ever mean the things you
use to say
I am at the point that it was all a game
you played
Never serious
But you will not make me delirious
with pain that you can't erase

If you search in your mind
The kiss was simple, a peck a kind
gesture at most
Nothing more nothing less
From a patient that I had to see in
private because of your mess

Mess of accusations, constant
badgering and lies

That even my clients
Come to me in disguise
And you
Damn you

For taking something so real and raping
it with your illusions
Of mistrust and confusion
I just don't get how you couldn't see
That you are, well were my reality

That girl that you saw
I saved her life behind your back
And when I saw you standing there
I couldn't do anything but glare
At you with disgust and dismay

Because at that very moment I realized
That you didn't trust me at all
You followed me life a thief in the night
Now think long and hard and tell me
who's wrong and who's right?

SHATTERED BUT NOT BROKEN ~
Lonely Thoughts Chapter 17

DEEP RIVERS

Somewhere in all this mess

we both have digressed to a place

of I don't even know

The struggle of getting pass so much
hurt

The pain that resides in the two of us

and at times I can only focus on my own

Pain

and more

Pain

See I love this man deeply

and with ever fiber of my being

I want to make it work

More than just work

To be the relationship we both deserve

but I ask myself

Can it really be?

SHATTERED NOT BROKEN ~ Can We
Talk

Chapter 18

DEEP RIVERS

I made it to a safe place so that my tears could
flow down my face tears that could not stop I tried
to bring a halt to the emotions that had been kicked
into over drive

the stimulation that ran down my spine pass my
heart as you had thrown it away I don't know who
was more disgusted you or I at this point I believe
that it was a shared plan

One that I could definitely cancel return to sender
So I ask myself what now? See the reality was that
even though you discarded my heart my soul was
still attached to the one that was forever and
always

So I allowed the tears to flow and until there was
no dry eye and left with what to do where do I start
and then I realized that you and I was still what
exactly I didn't know but I do know to move forward
what was on the table needed my attention

so I sat down and I wrote a letter to the one that
held me one day and I knew then that at that
moment I could release the hold that I had on my
heart and allow him to become its new protector

I truly believe that nothing is ever done unless you
put the nail in the coffin sealed shut for eternity well
you are my infinity so that means we have work to
do

you have to fix what is broken and I have to allow
the process to be more than just a token of
sometime love we have to be all the time or the
hammer and nail sit on the shelf available for use

trust is not a one way highway and my time is more
valuable than an occasional let's try we are walking
in darkness as the sun lost in the sky I know where
to start but I can't start by myself

Can we talk?

KING

Ring ring ring, Hello beautiful just received your
message and talking to you is always a blessing

The safe haven is a quiet place bringing serene
moments that can never be erased for I heard your
tears through the writing of your soul and I asked
myself, King; can you make her rivers whole

I touched the paper as it was your face as my own
tears became real just to match yours slowly
tracing the outlines of my cheeks I paused....and
wanted to tell you that I still believe

I have never been a Master Craft Artist pottery
never been a hobby that I wanted to learn but you
asked me to fix these shallow walls of discontent
so I will learn with grace and truth for us in how to
reinvent

I will take the hammer and build up the tissues that
are issues sweat and toil all night long until I am
through for the same way you feel the need to
convince me of this truth I want to say a few things
to you

Your luggage became an empty suitcase as you
walk out my baggage became so heavy as I sat
here filled with doubt and I questions not our love
but our determination we are suppose to be two
hearts under One love Nation

I cried probably more than one man can stand I
punched silent walls and slammed visible doors
just trying to open up nailed windows of your
absence and close my mind to any hopeless
possibilities

This is written with a little of fear of losing you fully
so I am packing a bag to travel to your tears with

nothing but authority and power to hold you and I
am praying that God keeps the best part of you

Until our tears kiss and our souls revive I am
coming baby, to bring you back to life save some
tears for me to dry with my cloth tie a knot at the
end of the rope and hold on

SHATTERED BUT NOT BROKEN ~ THE
TURNAROUND
Chapter 19

DEEP RIVERS

Let's start with the simple things
Rewind back to the basics
and all that has been forgotten
when somewhere along this traveled road
I took you
You took me
and We took life for granted
Picking up only the pieces that carry weight
the weight that can help to rebuild the foundation
that we exploded on impact with the baggage that
should have been gone
long long time ago
we dressed it up and at the end of the day
it is still the same old luggage
I know that in the new walk
I want to talk
not at but to each other and that is not at the
beginning
it has to be beginning middle and eternity
if not
let's work on just being friends
and to do that, there is still work that needs to be
done
first, I am not nor will I ever be passing the time by
when in it, I give my all

the tears that flowed cleansed all that was
so that I could give all
if that is the path we venture
I want to be that ear that you whisper to
not the silent treatment as you know words
mean nothing without action
so silence means the car has stopped
and it is not in the driveway
far away from where it should
let's play in the rain
run through each others thoughts when not in
the presence of each other
finish each others thoughts
we have passed finishing a statement
I want to be your mistress
and love it
as you will be my hidden secret
and love it
walking hand in hand and we haven't left the couch
to do different than what was done before
no need to blame the other as
only a fool argues with themselves
to learn from and mend
healing two hearts
we will become better than ever before
or the best damn friends to die for
but we will do what needs to be done
to build a foundation that only we can be held
accountable for
we did the damage
so what amazing can we do?

KING

The days where the beginnings that shaped us like
a new novel
I read the first chapter in my early morning heart
meditation
and I notice the imperfections that I show for so
long
and I finally understood the reasons why we were
shattered and not strong
The pain that seemed so inhumane and the words
that was smeared
as two hearts became damaged in a moment's
notice
the quest was a journey and it is still unfilled
gathering our hearts like sour grapes in a open
field
How can you fix your lips to be my mistress?
how can I ever be your best kept secret?
I feel offended by such a gesture
I guess I will call Ma'am and you can call me Sir
I see through your smooth but friendly word play
I am so past the silly little blame game
if we are going to fully get off the fence and mend
then this little advice I have to lend
Tell me that you love me and really care
for I am deeply pained by this life we shared
I want to romance you and not break into your
heart
the car has stopped because we need to finally
restart
Kiss me and show me the desire that created us

read me a book on our couch that we sat on
without lust
let eternal flow once again to the making of love
the scar tissue has to be gone under sea water
below
Amazing only starts with unconditional forgiveness
I need your grace within this season
so when I feel rain it doesn't matter cause your are
there
you will be amazing enough with the love you wear

SHATTERED NOT BROKEN~SHATTERED
MINUTES ~ CRITICAL PIECES
Chapter 20

KING

The ride to the hospital in the rain
was long, draining and very emotional
the tears was deeper than the depth of hell
the words on the phone made my heart fail
My mind went back to our first kiss
our last summer night walk under the moon
the way we converse as we talk
and there was no worries if we had any faults
The jog to the hospital doors from the dreary
parking lot
had a storm brewing inside me tossing my mind in
a whirlwind
people looked like witches on flying brooms
all I wanted with a heavy heart was to get to my
baby's room

The nurses station seemed like gates - bars on a
prison cell
as the precious women that I viewed as
Correctional Officer
asked me questions that I cared not to give a retort
I just wanted the directions to Emergency Room
door
I felt I was chewing on glass
swallowing my own vomit
punched by my own hands

my mind is in a football blitzs.....I DON'T
UNDERSTAND!!!!

As I sat in the waiting room feeling defeated as a
man
I wanted to go to the store instead being in bed
holding her hand
the faith, the hope and the prayer that I privately
speak
caused me to doubt and not even get on my knees
Three hours seemed like forever and five months
as the doctor walked the Green Mile to get to me
I braced myself for the pain that griped my life
I just want to hear the voice of my......beautiful wife
His words was like a howling wolf as he spoke
telling how she lost so much of her royal blood
"the next few hours are critical to her very
existence", he said
as I sat shattered, broken and in pieces...I...waited
to listen...

DEEP RIVERS

I laid in a place that was foreign
the pain that I felt was beyond worn
deeper than a woman scorn

My body betrayed me as it could not be mine
My screams could not be heard
I cringed at the laughter around me
Grimacing at the sound of his voice
and the woman he spoke with

And nothing I did in my head
happened in reality
What the hell is going on, what happened
My last recollection is hearing the words I love you

The voice that I know
seems to disgrace me as I try to move
speak, scream or even whisper
and nothing happens

WHAT THE HELL HAPPEN?

As the doors opens and I know I am not
cannot be hearing what I think I am hearing
I have literally been here how long?
Did he just say 2 months?

What?
Who?
How in the hell?

She must remain in this coma until the swelling
goes down
The voices made choices about my life
and as if I was not laying 2 feet away from them
Why had I been betrayed
Love that he proclaimed but I was betrayed
and then

I heard his voice say
No way
I thought I heard his laugh
I know I smell his scent
and I hit replay

He said as long as she is here
I will remain by her side
leaving only to put on her favorite cologne
so that she knows

Her eyes may not open but she knows
she may not be able to move
but she knows I hold and caress her hands
I brush her hair daily just so she knows I'm here

Rain on an icy road almost took
what I fought so hard to find
and I will not mind
one moment that I spend waiting for her to return

What I thought was my mind caught in the
madness

of me
What I found was even though I was broken and
shattered
I was not alone
My husband never left my side
Two souls that would heal together

Love heals more than any drug ever will....

SHATTERED BUT NOT BROKEN ~ If You
Can
Chapter 21

KING

Baby, if you will
and if you can
dismiss my faults
and please understand
for you know my pain
You know the truth
you can also gather all the facts
but please do not reprimand me
you know I am not a perfect man
so, I ask you to come and take my hand
It's your strength of love
that banishes all my pain

Yes, you can have all my brokenness
the ones that I never shared
I cannot hide from this burden
I am shattered and my eyes are finally sore
I cannot say if tomorrow will ever come
I can't even go on
therefore, I lay at your feet these tiny
fragments
the crippling lies that has disabled us

So, if you can
and if you will
blot out my past
erase my faults
and see I am just a human
I know each time I mess up

I look for your hand
you kiss my tears and let me stand
I may never see everything you may see
but I am not blind and I will walk the path
even though I don't have the right to say
can you take me back once again

So, if you will
and if you can
squeeze as you take my hand
and hug me to relieve me from this rain
the storm is strong no shelter from this pain
please look past this outer shell
for I don't like living in this shame
let me get soaked by your love
let it pour deep into my soul
so, if you will
and if you can
I know you know the facts
so please take my hand...take my hand

DEEP RIVERS

The storm that continues to lay upon us
moments that never seem to stay right
before they go left
yes I know what you say but I have heard it
before
tears that I have seen so many times
I am broken just as you are
maybe even more
reality has not dealt me an easy hand
and even then I keep moving
My issue is how long do we have stay in the
middle of this storm
When will you stop walking sideways in a
backwards world
Or will you continue to
Only time will tell
My biggest fear is am I out of time
Do you see the scars that no longer heal
My tears that no longer fall
lost in the storm with the thought
That I don't want to be rescued
And then it hit me
No matter the situation or the storm that we
are in
We seem to be in it together
You may not always be there at the
beginning
but you do see it through the end
I take your hand and walk forward
Not backwards
Seeing more than a light
Purpose with a plan

Yes I take your hand as you take mine
We shall do this together.......

SHATTERED BUT BROKEN ~ And She
Said Yes
Chapter 22

KING

I was in derision in how to present my
request
the dreadful days of yesterday
relationships
the sad times of if I am ready for this
brand of love
then I thought, yes she is more than
enough
I carefully examine myself and my
motives
was I ready to finally give up my
womanizing ways
to fully comprehend the totality of my
final resting place
in the bosom of love that was created in
my face
She asked me, will I always be there for
her?
that is when I pulled out the ring and to
ask
will you marry me?; and have me
forever and a day
And She Said Yes! and my heart knew
the Amazing Grace
This is not the story line to a fictional

situation
for the main characters have made the
curtain call
and the lights was dimmed on the faces
of two bright stars
ready to dance in the moonlight in new
found love

So, I gathered my thoughts as I walked
into another room
I missed her presence that quick and
now I know love again
it is amazing in how life evolves in a full
circle of newness
and a brand new start is now right back
at the beginning
When the beauty meets the beast
and the princess kisses the frog
a fairly tale becomes more than a soap
opera
it becomes hand fitting into a warm
customized glove
The gleam in her eyes even though the
ring didn't fit
the glitter of precious gems in a smile
that is not dim
for when your hand is put in mine and
we loudly proclaim I Do
we finally are ready to hang our own
sensual moon
Teary eyes will stare at the fulfillment of

this cherished moment
love has a purpose with a defining
meaning
that grasp the heart and consoles of
yesterday pain
all because, She Said Yes to this our
love has changed her name

DEEP RIVERS

Many that have followed this fairy tale
that at times was far from that
assumed that we had already tied the
knot
it seemed liked it
I know we have put in the time
The legalities of it all never got that far
Even when my heart was there a long
time ago
I just had to wait for him to catch up
I believe he finally has
The accident was more than a wake up
call
It was the second chance that most
never get
I heard a voice that I never heard before
The voice of love that was stronger than
all the years
I listened to the voice of love and knew
That we not me
Was given another chance to really get
it right
and my promise was, we would
Now he could not hear me as I was in a
coma
but I knew then
I know now
and will forever know
That even though we both made

mistakes
We were meant to be together
Meant for each other
Ride or die
To death do us part
That I doubted in the past
But never again will I have doubt
I said yes
Not to our past but to what the future
holds
For us
From this day forth......

SHATTERED NOT BROKEN ~ Staying
through Promises

Chapter 23

King

I took you on a ride of hopelessness and unfulfilled
promises
but yet you loved me in my brokenness
you kept a faith that was hard to sustain
that is I had to brandish you with my name

My eyes were dried by soft loving hands

you brought the best out of me through your
patience

I did not always say the best words to you

in my imperfection you loved me even though I
was a damn fool

Your silent corner was your safe haven from me

I knew many nights you prayed that you would be
free

but you stayed and loved me anyways baby

I don't even have the right phrases

I know I hurt your heart and not your face

I know that I mingled your feelings that cannot be
erased

to ignored the punctures that I placed in your soul

is like being in the dark and falling into a black hole

I never gangster thugged you because I was not
afraid to love

you showed me that it was alright to put my gun

to believe in myself even though it took sometime
to see

I am more grateful today that you stayed and did
not leave

I love the feet that I hold at night

that stood with me through this test of time

I adore the hands that I hold when we go on our
walks

when I look into your eyes I ripped off the disguise
and ....talk

Therefore, when I kiss you now it has so much of a
profound meaning

not because you are my wife but because you
taught me to love you

as a person and as a woman with high respect

sweet love, you haven't seen the best in me yet

Now fix me some of your good tasting Gumbo

I will feed you from my hands as my heart watch
me feed you

everyday with you will always be a special day of
grace

I want to thank you my love, for loving me anyways

DEEP RIVERS

I listen to your words

I hear pass the sound and through the hurt

but this was not just you

I held my place in this battle we have called life

for so long

the ups and downs of the roller coasters we rode

never really knowing when the ride would end

and when it did

a strange pull came over me and yes instead of

walking away, getting off the damn ride

I went for yet another turn

see I was not in this all alone

as you were not alone either

even when I felt stranded on a desert island

my pain took over but my memories seem to ride
off in the sunset

ahead of all the rest

so I stayed

and I stayed

and stayed

and now

we have to write a better chapter because the keys
have

worn out

with where we have been

I know now more than I thought back then

and with the turn of the times we can

be all that we have tried for so many years

the chance to get it right

hitting the mark of love

because we finally are walking hand in hand....

I ask that you forgive me as I have forgiven you

to learn from

not forget

were we came from

and to plan the best future we can

to were we are going

SHATTERED NOT BROKEN ~ The Anniversary

Chapter 24

KING

I am going to ask you this one time "who is this guy
that I saw you hugging last night?"
I was riding by the Art Gallery
I was on my way to Macys to pick up your gift for
our anniversary

My mind keeps having snapshots of that embrace

the informal photograph is now framed upon my
heart

a quick shot was taken without deliberate aim

and I question in that moment was you feelings still
the same

My heart captured everything from the silent sound

to the unwanted release by you both

the seat belt became my concrete prison

that would not release me

in all of this confusion

As I sat glued to this contraption of a chained
debate

the state of being without the necessaries of life
call you

was ripping my thought process in to tiny shreds

my soul became scared and once again afraid

I tried to erased the notion that it was nothing but a simple hug

that he must of been just a long time friend

but it's something about the release that was in suspension

the care and the concern was deeper than my comprehension

As I pulled away from what I considered a crime scene

We been through so much in our short lives

The bumps, the bruises and being forsaken

Being shattered and ever so broken

I love you so deeply with all that is within me

I couldn't dismiss this so I just had to ask you

I am asking through hurt lips and a scarred mind

Our communication is on a new level that is so high

I am a guitar just ready to be strummed by your hands

Rest your fingers on the fret bar of my soul

Let the music that you play be sweet music

Happy Anniversary baby, you have been worth it

DEEP RIVERS

First let me say that I am glad that you asked
Instead of
Doing what
Just like always
You asked and I know we have progressed from
where we were
to where we are
another level of our relationship

I have wanted to tell you this for so long wait......I
don't know if I can I want to ......I have to and
....breathe.....you can do this

All this time I put up with accusations

other women

mess after mess with you

not knowing if we would survive

hell, at times I didn't want to survive but I ..... just
couldn't let go

The hurt and the pain

continued to grow and you continued to water it

no room for it to die just like I wanted to....die over
and over again but you would not let me go...

you had a hold on my heart

strapped my emotions beneath you and suffocated
my spirit and I still couldn't let go....walk away

So the man you saw me hugging was my help

my lifeline

my listening ear

my reasoning

my life jacket

See through it all I was broken

no I wasn't shattered

but I was broken

and I still held on

but the blessing was I am a counselor

so I knew

I couldn't counsel myself

I found someone

that could and would

He was the right to my wrong

the up from the down

and when all else had failed

he found hope

not in me but in you

see I told him every little nugget about us

and when I was at my worse

he found good in you to bring me back

See the issue was he knew I wouldn't leave you

so he helped me to stay

what I didn't see

he showed me through his eyes

but it was you that I saw

he took all the bad in you and outweighed it with
the good

He said if you are going to stay

you need to strip away the layers to see

what can be

not to allow all the negative to live your life

and the positive to move in

So do you see reason of concern with that hug

yes you did

the reason was me

I wasn't sure I was ready

strong enough to make it work

and when he held me

he whispered

whenever you want to worry just remember

you both were broken but neither was shattered so
yes you can do it.....

enjoy your blessings.....and I am here if the two of
you ever need me....

Happy anniversary love.....you have been worth it

BIO: King Judah

I am a writer that goes by the pen name King Judah. One that believes in the power of romance. I have been a writer now for the past seventeen (17) years and I have really emerge myself in love. Writing from experience and writing from the perspective of what love and romance can be.

When Love and Romance kisses each other it brings about a feeling that is surreal and not complicated. Allow yourself to be loved by you so you can love others as partners, friends and companions. I love to give men that voice, that opportunity that it is alright to express that natural and vulnerable said to the one that you love everyday.

Bio Deep Rivers:

Dawn Blanchard with her writing partner and friend Steven Lester collaborated on a business venture idea to establish Left Thought Films and Left Thought Media that houses two (2) Publishing Companies, Vantage Point Publishing and Amorous Ink. She offers Poets, Writers and Dreamers like herself whom are often overlooked, discounted or overshadowed by larger publishing companies, a vehicle to showcase their works.

Dawn's vision acknowledges the strength, core values and necessity to return back to the basic foundation of "WORDS". One of her infamous prose is "Without Words We All Live In Silence" thus no Books, no Radio and no Scripts! You can reach me at deeprivers67@yahoo.com, 317-418-2076

www.ingramcontent.com/pod-product-compliance
Lightning Source LLC
Chambersburg PA
CBHW032049180726
48284CB00004B/1246